Comfort Pease
&
Her Gold Ring

Mary Eleanor Wilkins Freeman

COMFORT PEASE AND HER GOLD RING

One of the first things which Comfort remembered being told was that she had been named for her Aunt Comfort, who had given her a gold ring and a gold dollar for her name. Comfort could not understand why. It always seemed to her that her aunt, and not she, had given the name, and that she should have given the ring and the dollar; but that was what her mother had told her. "Your Aunt Comfort gave you this beautiful gold ring and this gold dollar for your name," said she.

The ring and the dollar were kept in Mrs. Pease's little rosewood work-box, which she never used for needlework, but as a repository for her treasures. Her best cameo brooch was in there, too, and a lock of hair of Comfort's baby brother who died.

One of Comfort's chiefest delights was looking at her gold ring and gold dollar. When she was very good her mother would unlock the rosewood box and let her see them. She had never worn the ring—it was much too large for her. Aunt Comfort and her mother had each thought that it was foolish to buy a gold ring that she could outgrow. "If it was a chameleon ring I wouldn't care," said Aunt Comfort; "but it does seem a pity when it's a real gold ring." So the ring was bought a little too large for Comfort's mother. She was a very small woman, and Comfort was a large baby, and, moreover, favored her father's family, who were all well grown, and Aunt Comfort feared she might have larger fingers.

"Why, I've seen girls eight years old with fingers a good deal bigger than yours, Emily," she said. "Suppose Comfort shouldn't be able to get that ring on her finger after she's eight years old, what a pity 'twould be, when it's real gold, too!"

But when Comfort was eight years old she was very small for her age, and she could actually crowd two of her fingers—the little one and the third—into the ring. She begged her mother to let her wear it so, but she would not. "No," said she, "I sha'n't let you make yourself a laughing-stock by wearing a ring any such way as that. Besides, you couldn't use your fingers. You've got to wait till your hand grows to it."

So poor little Comfort waited, but she had a discouraged feeling sometimes that her hand never would grow to it. "Suppose I shouldn't be any bigger than you, mother," she said, "couldn't I ever wear the ring?"

"Hush! you will be bigger than I am. All your father's folks are, and you look just like them," said her mother, conclusively, and Comfort tried to have faith. The gold dollar also could only impart the simple delight of possession, for it was not to be spent. "I am going to give her a gold dollar to keep beside the ring," Aunt Comfort had said.

"What is it for?" Comfort asked sometimes when she gazed at it shining in its pink cotton bed in the top of the work-box.

"It's to keep," answered her mother.

Comfort grew to have a feeling, which she never expressed to anybody, that her gold dollar was somehow like Esau's birthright, and something dreadful would happen to her if she parted with it. She felt safer, because a "mess of pottage" didn't sound attractive to her, and she did not think she would ever be tempted to spend her gold dollar for that.

Comfort went to school when she was ten years old. She had not begun as early as most of the other girls, because she lived three quarters of a mile from the school-house and had many sore throats. The doctors had advised her mother to teach her at home; and she could do that, because she had been a teacher herself when she was a girl.

Comfort had not been to school one day before everybody in it knew about her gold ring and her dollar, and it happened in this way: She sat on the bench between Rosy and Matilda Stebbins, and Rosy had a ring on the middle finger of her left hand. Rosy was a fair, pretty little girl, with long light curls, which all the other girls admired and begged for the privilege of twisting. Rosy at recess usually had one or two of her friends standing at her back twisting her soft curls over their fingers.

Rosy wore pretty gowns and aprons, too, and she was always glancing down to see if her skirt was spread out nicely when she sat on the bench. Her sister Matilda had just as pretty gowns, but she was not pretty herself. However, she was a better scholar, although she was a year younger. That day she kept glancing across Comfort at her sister, and her black eyes twinkled angrily.

Rosy sometimes sat with her left hand pressed affectedly against her pink cheek, with the ring-finger bent slightly outward; and then she held up her spelling-book before her with her left hand, and the same ostentatious finger.

Finally Matilda lost her patience, and she whispered across Comfort Pease. "You act like a ninny," said she to Rosy, with a fierce pucker of her red lips and a twinkle of her black eyes.

Rosy looked at her, and the pink spread softly all over her face and neck; but she still held her spelling-book high, and the middle finger with the ring wiggled at the back of it.

"It ain't anything but brass, neither," whispered Matilda.

"It ain't," Rosy whispered back.

"Smell of it."

Rosy crooked her arm around her face and began to cry. However, she cried quite easily, and everybody was accustomed to seeing her fair head bent over the hollow of her arm several times a day, so she created no excitement at all. Even the school-teacher simply glanced at her and said nothing. The school-teacher was an elderly woman who had taught school ever since she was sixteen. She was called very strict, and the little girls were all afraid of her. She could ferule a boy just as well as a man could. Her name was Miss Tabitha Hanks. She did not like Rosy Stebbins very well, although she tried to be impartial. Once at recess she pushed Charlotte Hutchins and Sarah Allen, who were twisting Rosy's curls, away, and gathered them all up herself in one hard hand. "I'd cut them all off if I were your mother," said she, with a sharp little tug; but when Rosy rolled her scared blue eyes up at her, she only laughed grimly and let go.

Now Miss Hanks just looked absently at Rosy weeping in the hollow of her blue gingham arm, then went over to the blackboard and began writing, in fair, large characters, "A rolling stone gathers no moss," for the scholars to copy in their copy-books. The temptation and the opportunity were too much for Comfort Pease. She nudged Matilda Stebbins and whispered in her ear, although she knew that whispering in school was wrong. "I've got a real gold ring," whispered Comfort.

Matilda turned astonished eyes upon her. "You ain't."

"Yes, I have."

"Who gave it to you?"

"My Aunt Comfort, for my name."

"Were you named for her?"

"Yes, and she gave me a real gold ring for it."

"Matilda Stebbins and Comfort Pease, stand out on the floor," said Miss Tabitha Hanks, sharply. Comfort gave a great jump—the teacher had been standing at the blackboard with her back toward them, and how had she seen? Never after that did Comfort feel quite safe from Miss Tabitha's eyes; even if they were on the other side of the wall she could not quite trust it.

"Step right out on the floor, Matilda and Comfort," repeated Miss Tabitha, and out the two little girls stepped. Comfort's knees shook, and she was quite pale. Matilda looked very sober, but her black eyes gave a defiant flash when she was out on the floor and saw that her sister Rosy had lowered her arm and was looking at her with gentle triumph. "You see what you've got because you called my ring brass," Rosy seemed to say; and Matilda gave a stern little nod at her, as if she replied, "It is brass."

Poor little Comfort did not feel much sustained by the possession of her real gold ring. It was dreadful to stand out there facing the school, which seemed to be a perfect dazzle of blue and black eyes all fastened upon her in her little red gown and gingham tier, in her little stout shoes, which turned in for very meekness, with her little dangling hands, which could not wear the gold ring, and her little strained face and whispering lips, and little vain heart, which was being punished for its little vanity.

They stood on the floor until recess. Comfort felt so weak and stiff that she could scarcely move when Miss Hanks said harshly, "Now you can go." She cast a piteous glance at Matilda, who immediately put her arms around her waist and pulled her along to the entry, where their hoods and cloaks hung. "Don't you cry," she whispered. "She's awful strict, but she won't hurt you a mite. She brought me a whole tumbler of currant jelly when I had the measles."

"I sha'n't whisper again as long as I live," half sobbed Comfort, putting on her hood.

"I sha'n't, either," said Matilda. "I never had to stand out on the floor before. I don't know what my mother will say when I tell her."

The two little girls went out in the snowy yard, and there was Rosy, with Charlotte Hutchins and Sarah Allen, and she was showing them her ring. It was again too much for sensible little Matilda, weary from her long stand on the floor. "Rosy Stebbins, you are a great ninny, acting so stuck up over that old brass ring," said she. "Comfort Pease has a real solid gold one, and she don't even wear it."

Rosy and Charlotte Hutchins and Sarah Allen all stared at Comfort. "Have you?" asked Charlotte Hutchins, in an awed tone. She was a doctor's daughter, and had many things that the other little girls had not; but even she had no gold ring—nothing but a chameleon.

"Yes, I have," replied Comfort, blushing modestly.

"Real gold?" asked Rosy, in a subdued voice.

"Yes."

Some other girls came up—some of the older ones, with their hair done up; and even some of the boys, towering lankily on the outskirts. Not one of these scholars in this country district school fifty years ago had ever owned a gold ring. All they had ever seen were their mothers' well-worn wedding-circlets.

"Comfort Pease has got a real gold ring," went from one to the other.

"Why don't she wear it, then?" demanded one of the big girls. She had very red cheeks, and her black hair was in two glossy braids, crossed and pinned at the back of her head, and surmounted by her mother's shell comb she had let her wear to school that day. She had come out to recess without her hood to show it.

"She's waiting for her hand to grow to it," explained Matilda, to whom Comfort had shyly whispered the whole story.

"Hold up your hand," ordered the big girl; and Comfort held up her little hand pink with the cold.

"H'm! looks big enough," said the big girl, and she adjusted her shell comb.

"I call it a likely story," said another big girl, in an audible whisper.

"The Peases don't have any more than other folks," said still another big girl. The little crowd dispersed with scornful giggles. Comfort turned redder and redder. Rosy and Charlotte and Sarah were looking at her curiously; only Matilda stood firm. "You are all just as mean as you can be!" she cried. "She has got a gold ring!"

Matilda Stebbins put her arm around Comfort, who was fairly crying. "Come," said she, "don't you mind anything about 'em, Comfort. Le'ss go in the school-house. I've got a splendid Baldwin apple in my dinner-pail, and I'll give you half of it. They're mad 'cause they haven't got any gold ring."

"I have got a gold ring," sobbed Comfort:

 "Honest and true,
Black and blue,
Lay me down and cut me in two."

That was the awful truth-testing formula of the village children.

"Course you have," said Matilda, with indignant backward glances at the others. "Le'ss go and get that Baldwin apple."

Comfort went with Matilda; but it took more than a Baldwin apple to solace her; and her first day at school was a most unhappy one. It was very probable that the other scholars, and especially the elder ones, who had many important matters of their own in mind, thought little more about her and her gold ring after school had begun; but Comfort could not understand that. She had a feeling that the minds of the whole school were fixed upon her, and she was standing upon a sort of spiritual platform of shame, which was much worse than the school-room floor. If she saw one girl whisper to another, she directly thought it was about her. If a girl looked at her, her color rose, and her heart began to beat loudly, for she thought she was saying to herself, "Likely story!"

Comfort was thankful when it was time to go home, and she could trudge off alone down the snowy road. None of the others lived her way. She left them all at the turn of the road just below the school-house.

"Good-night, Comfort," Matilda Stebbins sang out loyally; but the big girl with red cheeks followed her with, "Wear that gold ring to school to-morrow, an' let us see it." Then everybody giggled, and poor Comfort fled out of sight. It seemed to her that she must wear that ring to school the next day. She made up her mind that she would ask her mother; but when she got home she found that her Grandmother Atkins had come, and also her Uncle Ebenezer and Aunt Susan. They had driven over from Barre, where they lived, and her grandmother was going to stay and make a little visit; but her uncle and aunt were going home soon, and her mother was hurrying to make some hot biscuits for supper.

So when Comfort came in she stopped short at the sight of the company, and had to kiss them all and answer their questions with shy politeness. Comfort was very fond of her grandmother, but this time she did not feel quite so delighted to see her as usual. As soon as she had got a chance she slipped into the pantry after her mother. "Mother," she whispered, pulling her apron softly, "can't I wear my gold ring to school to-morrow?"

"No, you can't. How many times have I got to tell you?" said her mother, mixing her biscuit dough energetically.

"Please let me, mother. They didn't believe I've got one."

"Let them believe it or not, just as they have a mind to," said her mother.

"They think I'm telling stories."

"What have you been telling about your ring in school for, when you ought to have been studying? Now, Comfort, I can't have you standing there teasing me any longer. I've got to get these biscuits into the oven; they must have some supper before they go home. You go right out and set the table. Get the clean table-cloth out of the drawer, and you may put on the best knives and forks. Not another word. You can't wear that gold ring until your hand grows to it, and that settles it."

Comfort went out and set the table, but she looked so dejected that the company all noticed it. She could not eat any of the hot biscuits when they sat down to supper, and she did not eat much of the company cake. "You don't feel sick, do you, child?" asked her grandmother, anxiously.

"No, ma'am," replied Comfort, and she swallowed a big lump in her throat.

"She ain't sick," said her mother, severely. "She's fretting because she can't wear her gold ring to school."

"O Comfort, you must wait till your hand grows to it," said her Aunt Susan.

"Yes, of course she must," said her Uncle Ebenezer.

"Eat your supper, and your hand will grow to it before long," said her father, who, left to himself, would have let Comfort wear the ring.

"It wouldn't do for you to wear that ring and lose it. It's real gold," said her grandmother. "Have another piece of the sweet-cake."

But Comfort wanted no more sweet-cake. She put both hands to her face and wept, and her mother sent her promptly out of the room and to bed. Comfort lay there and sobbed, and heard her Uncle Ebenezer's covered wagon roll out of the yard, and sobbed again. Then she fell asleep, and did not know it when her mother and grandmother came in and looked at her and kissed her.

"I'm sorry she feels so bad," said Comfort's mother, "but I can't let her wear that ring."

"No, you can't," said her grandmother. And they went out shading the candle.

Comfort said no more about the ring the next morning. She knew her mother too well. She did not eat much breakfast, and crept off miserably to school at a quarter past eight, and she had another unhappy day. Nobody had forgotten about the gold ring. She was teased about it at every opportunity. "Why didn't you wear that handsome gold ring?" asked the big girl with red cheeks, until poor Comfort got nearly distracted. It seemed to her that the time to go home would never come, and as if she could never endure to go to school again. That night she begged her mother to let her stay at home the next day. "No," said her mother; "you've begun to go to school, and you're going to school unless you're sick. Now this evening you had better sit down and write a letter to your Aunt Comfort. It's a long time since you wrote to her."

So Comfort sat down and wrote laboriously a letter to her Aunt Comfort, and thanked her anew, as she always did, for her gold ring and the gold dollar. "I wish to express my thanks again for the beautiful and valuable gifts which you presented me for my name," wrote Comfort, in the little stilted style of the day.

After the letter was written it was eight o'clock, and Comfort's mother said she had better go to bed.

"You look tired out," said she; "I guess you'll have to go to bed early if you're going to school."

"Can't I stay home to-morrow, mother?" pleaded Comfort, with sudden hope.

"No," said her mother; "you've got to go if you're able."

"Mother, can't I wear it just once?"

"Don't you bring that ring up again," said her mother. "Take your candle and go right upstairs."

Comfort gave a pitiful little sob.

"Now don't you go to crying over it," ordered her mother; and Comfort tried to choke back another sob as she went out of the room.

Comfort's father looked up from the Old Farmer's Almanac. He was going to Bolton the next day with a load of wood, and wanted to see what the weather would be, and so was consulting the almanac.

"What was it Comfort wanted?" he inquired.

"She wanted to wear that gold ring her Aunt Comfort gave her to school," replied Mrs. Pease. "And I've told her over and over again I shouldn't let her do it."

"It's a mile too big for her, and she'd be sure to lose it off," said Grandmother Atkins; "and it would be a pity to have anything happen to it, when it's real gold, too."

"She couldn't wind a rag round her finger under it, could she?" asked Comfort's father, hesitatingly.

"Wear a rag round her finger under it!" repeated Mrs. Pease. "I rather guess she can wait till her finger grows to it. You'd let that child do anything."

Mr. Pease did not say anything more, but studied the Old Farmer's Almanac again, and found out it was likely to be fair weather for the season.

It was past midnight, and the hearth fire was raked down, and Comfort's father and mother and grandmother were all in bed and asleep, when a little figure in a white nightgown, holding a lighted candle, padding softly on little cold bare feet, came down the stairs. Comfort paused in the entry and listened. She could hear the clock tick and her father snore. The best parlor door was on the right. She lifted the brass catch cautiously, and pushed the door open. Then she stole into the best parlor. The close, icy air smote her like a breath from the north pole. There was no fire in the best parlor except on Thanksgiving day, and perhaps twice besides, when there was company to tea, from fall to spring. The cold therein seemed condensed and concentrated; the haircloth sofa and chairs and the mahogany table seemed to give out cold as stoves did heat.

There were two coffin-plates and funeral wreaths, which had belonged to the uncles of Comfort who had died before she was born, in frames on the wall, and these always scared Comfort.

She kept her eyes away from them as she went swiftly on her little bare feet, which had no feeling in them as they pressed the icy floor, across to the mahogany card-table, whereon was set the rosewood work-box.

Comfort set her candle on the table, and turned the key of the box with her stiff fingers. Then she raised the lid noiselessly, and there lay the ring in a little square compartment of the tray. Next to it, in the corner square, lay the gold dollar.

Comfort took the ring out, shut the box-lid down, turned the key, and fled. She thought some one called her name as she went upstairs, and she stopped and listened; but all she heard was the clock ticking and her father snoring and her heart beating. Then she kept on to her own chamber, and put out her candle, and crept into her feather-bed under the patchwork quilts. There she lay all night, wide awake, with the gold ring clasped tightly in her little cold fist.

When Comfort came downstairs the next morning there was a bright red spot on each cheek, and she was trembling as if she had a chill.

Her mother noticed it, and asked if she was cold, and Comfort said, "Yes, ma'am."

"Well, draw your stool up close to the fire and get warm," said her mother. "Breakfast is 'tmost ready. You can have some of the pancakes to carry to school for your dinner."

Comfort sat soberly in the chimney-corner until breakfast was ready, as her mother bade her. She was very silent, and did not say anything during breakfast unless some one asked her a question.

When she started for school her mother and grandmother stood in the window and watched her.

It was a very cold morning, and Mrs. Pease had put her green shawl on Comfort over her coat; and the little girl looked very short and stout as she trudged along between the snow-ridges which bordered the path, and yet there was a forlorn air about her.

"I don't know as the child was fit to go to school to-day," Mrs. Pease said, doubtfully.

"She didn't look very well, and she didn't eat much breakfast, either," said Grandmother Atkins.

"She was always crazy after hot pancakes, too," said her mother.

"Hadn't you better call her back, Em'ly?"

"No, I won't," said Mrs. Pease, turning away from the window. "She's begun to go to school, and I'm not going to take her out unless I'm sure she ain't able to go."

So Comfort Pease went on to school; and she had the gold ring in her pocket, which was tied around her waist with a string under her dress skirt, as was the fashion then. Comfort often felt of the pocket to be sure the ring was safe as she went along. It was bitterly cold; the snow creaked under her stout shoes. Besides the green shawl, her red tippet was wound twice around her neck and face; but her blue eyes peering over it were full of tears which the frosty wind forced into them, and her breath came short and quick. When she came in sight of the school-house she could see the straight column of smoke rising out of the chimney, it was so thin in the cold air. There were no scholars out in the yard, only a group coming down the road from the opposite direction. It was too cold to play out of doors before school, as usual.

Comfort pulled off her mittens, thrust her hand in her pocket dangling against her blue woolen petticoat, and drew out the gold ring.

Then she slipped it on over the third and fourth fingers of her left hand, put her mittens on again, and went on.

It was quite still in the school-house, although school had not begun, because Miss Tabitha Hanks had arrived. Her spare form, stiff and wide, and perpendicular as a board, showed above the desk. She wore a purple merino dress buttoned down the front with dark black buttons, and a great breastpin of twisted gold. Her hair was looped down over her ears in two folds like shiny drab satin. It scarcely looked like hair, the surface was so smooth and unbroken; and a great tortoise-shell comb topped it like a coronet.

Miss Tabitha's nose was red and rasped with the cold; her thin lips were blue, and her bony hands were numb; but she set copies in writing-books with stern patience. Not one to yield to a little fall in temperature was Tabitha Hanks. Moreover, she kept a sharp eye on the school, and she saw every scholar who entered, while not seeming to do so.

She saw Comfort Pease when she came shyly in, and at once noticed something peculiar about her. Comfort wore the same red tibet dress and the same gingham apron that she had worn the day before; her brown hair was combed off her high, serious forehead and braided in the same smooth tails; her blue eyes looked abroad in the same sober and timid fashion; and yet there was a change.

Miss Tabitha gave a quick frown and a sharp glance of her gray eyes at her, then she continued setting her copy. "That child's up to something," she thought, while she wrote out in her beautiful shaded hand, "All is not gold that glitters."

Comfort went forward to the stove, which was surrounded by a ring of girls and boys. Matilda Stebbins and Rosy were there with the rest. Matilda moved aside at once when she saw Comfort, and made room for her near the stove.

"Hullo, Comfort Pease!" said she.

"Hullo!" returned Comfort.

Comfort held out her numb right hand to the stove, but the other she kept clenched in a little blue fist hidden in her dress folds.

"Cold, ain't it?" said Matilda.

"Dreadful," said Comfort, with a shiver.

"Why don't you warm your other hand?" asked Matilda.

"My other hand ain't cold," said Comfort. And she really did not think it was. She was not aware of any sensation in that hand, except that of the gold ring binding together the third and fourth fingers.

Pretty soon the big girl with red cheeks came in. Her cheeks were redder than ever, and her black eyes seemed to have caught something of the sparkle of the frost outside. "Hullo!" said she, when she caught sight of Comfort. "That you, Comfort Pease?"

"Hullo!" Comfort returned, faintly. She was dreadfully afraid of this big girl, who was as much as sixteen years old, and studied algebra, and was also said to have a beau.

"Got that gold ring" inquired the big girl, with a giggle, as she held out her hands to the stove.

Comfort looked at her as if she was going to cry.

"You're real mean to tease her, so there!" said Matilda Stebbins, bravely, in the face of the big girl, who persisted nevertheless.

"Got that gold ring?" she asked again, with her teasing giggle, which the others echoed.

Comfort slowly raised her left arm. She unfolded her little blue fist, and there on the third and fourth fingers of her hand shone the gold ring.

Then there was such an outcry that Miss Tabitha Hanks looked up from her copy, and kept her wary eyes fixed upon the group at the stove.

"My sakes alive, look at Comfort Pease with a gold ring on two fingers!" screamed the big girl. And all the rest joined in. The other scholars in the room came crowding up to the stove. "Le'ss see it!" they demanded of Comfort. They teased her to let them take it. "Lemme take it for just a minute. I'll give it right back, honest," they begged. But Comfort was firm about that; she would not let that ring go from her own two fingers for one minute.

"Ain't she stingy with her old ring?" said Sarah Allen to Rosy Stebbins.

"Maybe it ain't real gold," whispered Rosy; but Comfort heard her.

"'Tis, too," said she, stoutly.

"It's brass; I can tell by the color," teased one of the big boys. "Fore I'd wear a brass ring if I was a girl!"

"It ain't brass," almost sobbed Comfort.

Miss Tabitha Hanks arose slowly and came over to the stove. She came so silently and secretly that the scholars did not notice it, and they all jumped when she spoke.

"You may all take your seats," said she, "if it is a little before nine. You can study until school begins. I can't have so much noise and confusion."

The scholars flocked discontentedly to their seats.

"It's all the fault of your old brass ring," whispered the big boy to Comfort, with a malicious grin, and she trembled.

"Your mother let you wear it, didn't she?" whispered Matilda to Comfort, as the two took their seats on the bench. But Comfort did not seem to hear her, and Miss Tabitha looked that way, and Matilda dared not whisper again. Miss Tabitha, moreover, looked as though she had heard what she said, although that did not seem possible.

However, Miss Tabitha's ears had a reputation among the scholars for almost as fabulous powers as her eyes. Matilda Stebbins was quite sure that she heard, and Miss Tabitha's after-course confirmed her opinion.

The reading-class was out on the floor fixing its toes on the line, and Miss Tabitha walked behind it straight to Comfort.

"Comfort Pease," said she, "I don't believe your mother ever sent you to school wearing a ring after that fashion. You may take it off."

Comfort took it off. The eyes of the whole school watched her; even the reading-class looked over its shoulders.

"Now," said Miss Tabitha, "put it in your pocket."

Comfort put the ring in her pocket. Her face was flushing redder and redder, and the tears rolled down her cheeks.

Miss Tabitha drew out a large pin, which was quilted into the bosom of her dress, and proceeded to pin up Comfort's pocket. "There," said she, "now you leave that ring in there, and don't you touch it till you go home; then you give it right to your mother. And don't you take that pin out; if you do I shall whip you."

Miss Tabitha turned suddenly on the reading-class, and the faces went about with a jerk. "Turn to the fifty-sixth page," she commanded; and the books all rustled open as she went to the front. Matilda gave Comfort a sympathizing poke and Miss Tabitha an indignant scowl under cover of the reading-class, but Comfort sat still, with the tears dropping down on her spelling-book. She had never felt so guilty or so humble in her life. She made up her mind she would tell her mother about it, and put the ring back in the box that night, and never take it out again until her finger grew to it; and if it never did she would try to be resigned.

When it was time for recess Miss Tabitha sent them all out of doors. "I know it's cold," said she, "but a little fresh air won't hurt any of you. You can run around and keep warm."

Poor Comfort dreaded to go out. She knew just how the boys and girls would tease her. But Matilda Stebbins stood by her, and the two hurried out before the others and ran together down the road.

"We've got time to run down to the old Loomis place and back before the bell rings," said Matilda. "If you stay here they'll all tease you dreadfully to show that ring, and if you do she'll whip you. She always does what she says she will."

The two girls got back to the school-house just as the bell rang, and, beyond sundry elbow-nudges and teasing whispers as they went in, Comfort had no trouble. She took her seat and meekly opened her geography.

Once in a while she wondered, with a qualm of anxiety, if her ring was safe. She dared not even feel of her pocket under her dress. Whenever she thought of it Miss Tabitha seemed to be looking straight at her. Poor Comfort had a feeling that Miss Tabitha could see her very thoughts.

The Stebbinses and Sarah Allen usually stayed at noon, but that day they all went home. Sarah Allen had company and the Stebbinses had a chicken dinner. So Comfort stayed alone. The other scholars lived near enough to the school-house to go home every day unless it was very stormy weather.

After everybody was gone, Miss Tabitha and all, the first thing Comfort did was to slide her hand down over the bottom of her pocket, and carefully feel of it under her dress skirt.

Her heart gave a great leap and seemed to stand still—she could not feel any ring there.

Comfort felt again and again, with trembling fingers. She could not believe that the ring was gone, but she certainly could not feel it. She was quite pale, and shook as if she had a chill. She was too frightened to cry. Had she lost Aunt

Comfort's ring—the real gold ring she had given her for her name? She looked at the pin which Miss Tabitha had quilted into the top of her pocket, but she dared not take it out. Suppose Miss Tabitha should ask if she had, and she had to tell her and be whipped? That would be almost worse than losing the ring.

Comfort had never been whipped in her life, and her blood ran cold at the thought of it.

She kept feeling wildly of the pocket. There was a little roll of writing-paper in it—some leaves of an old account-book which her mother had given her to write on. All the hope she had was that the ring had slipped inside that, and that was the reason why she could not feel it. She longed so to take out that pin and make sure, but she had to wait for that until she got home at night.

Comfort began to search all over the school-room floor, but all she found were wads of paper and apple-cores, slate-pencil stumps and pins. Then she went out in the yard and looked carefully, then she went down the road to the old Loomis place, where she and Matilda had walked at recess—Miss Tabitha Hanks went home that way—but no sign of the ring could she find. The road was as smooth as a white floor, too, for the snow was old and well trodden.

Comfort Pease went back to the school-house and opened her dinner-pail. She looked miserably at the pancakes, the bread and butter, and the apple-pie and cheese, and tried to eat, but she could not. She put the cover on the pail, leaned her head on the desk in front, and sat quite still until the scholars began to return. Then she lifted her head, got out her spelling-book, and tried to study. Miss Tabitha came back early, so nobody dared tease her; and the cold was so bitter and the sky so overcast that they were not obliged to go out at recess. Comfort studied and recited, and never a smile came on her pale, sober little face. Matilda whispered to know if she were sick, but Comfort only shook her head.

Sometimes Comfort saw Miss Tabitha watching her with an odd expression, and she wondered forlornly what it meant. She did not dream of going to Miss Tabitha with her trouble. She felt quite sure she would get no sympathy in that quarter.

All the solace Comfort had was that one little forlorn hope that the ring might be in that roll of paper, and she should find it when she got home.

It seemed to her that school never would be done. She thought wildly of asking Miss Tabitha if she could not go home because she had the toothache. Indeed, her tooth did begin to ache, and her head too; but she waited, and sped home like a rabbit when she was let out at last. She did not wait even to say a word to Matilda. Comfort, when she got home, went right through the sitting-room and upstairs to her own chamber.

"Where are you going, Comfort?" her mother called after her.

"What ails the child?" said Grandmother Atkins.

"I'm coming right back," Comfort panted as she fled.

The minute she was in her own cold little chamber she took the pin from her pocket, drew forth the roll of paper, and smoothed it out. The ring was not there. Then she turned the pocket and examined it. There was a little rip in the seam.

"Comfort, Comfort!" called her mother from the foot of the stairs. "You'll get your death of cold up there," chimed in her grandmother from the room beyond.

"I'm coming," Comfort gasped in reply. She turned the pocket back and went downstairs.

It was odd that, although Comfort looked so disturbed, neither her mother nor grandmother asked her what was the matter. They looked at her, then exchanged a meaning look with each other. And all her mother said was to bid her go and sit down by the fire and toast her feet. She also mixed a bowl of hot ginger-tea plentifully sweetened with molasses, and bade her drink that, so she could not catch cold; and yet there was something strange in her manner all the time. She made no remark, either, when she opened Comfort's dinner-pail and saw how little had been eaten. She merely showed it silently to Grandmother Atkins behind Comfort's back, and they nodded to each other with solemn meaning.

However, Mrs. Pease made the cream-toast that Comfort loved for supper, and obliged her to eat a whole plate of it.

"I can't have her get sick," she said to Grandmother Atkins after Comfort had gone to bed that night.

"She ain't got enough constitution, poor child," assented Grandmother Atkins.

Mrs. Pease opened the door and listened. "I believe she's crying now," said she. "I guess I'll go up there."

"I would if I was you," said Grandmother Atkins.

Comfort's sobs sounded louder and louder all the way, as her mother went upstairs.

"What's the matter, child?" she asked when she opened the door; and there was still something strange in her tone. While there was concern there was certainly no surprise.

"My tooth aches dreadfully," sobbed Comfort.

"You had better have some cotton-wool and paregoric on it, then," said her mother. Then she went downstairs for cotton-wool and paregoric, and she ministered to Comfort's aching tooth; but no cotton-wool or paregoric was there for Comfort's aching heart.

She sobbed so bitterly that her mother looked alarmed. "Comfort, look here; is there anything else the matter?" she asked, suddenly; and she put her hand on Comfort's shoulder.

"My tooth aches dreadfully—oh!" Comfort wailed.

"If your tooth aches so bad as all that, you'd better go to Dr. Hutchins in the morning and have it out," said her mother. "Now you'd better lie still and try to go to sleep, or you'll be sick."

Comfort's sobs followed her mother all the way downstairs. "Don't you cry so another minute, or you'll get so nervous you'll be sick," Mrs. Pease called back; but she sat down and cried awhile herself after she returned to the sitting-room.

Poor Comfort stifled her sobs under the patchwork quilt, but she could not stop crying for a long time, and she slept very little that night. When she did she dreamed that she had found the ring, but had to wear it around her aching tooth for a punishment, and the tooth was growing larger and larger, and the ring painfully tighter and tighter.

She looked so wan and ill the next morning that her mother told her she need not go to school. But Comfort begged hard to go, and said she did not feel sick; her tooth was better.

"Well, mind you get Miss Hanks to excuse you, and come home, if your tooth aches again," said her mother.

"Yes, ma'am," replied Comfort.

When the door shut behind Comfort her Grandmother Atkins looked at her mother. "Em'ly," said she, "I don't believe you can carry it out; she'll be sick."

"I'm dreadfully afraid she will," returned Comfort's mother.

"You'll have to tell her."

Mrs. Pease turned on Grandmother Atkins, and New England motherhood was strong in her face. "Mother," said she, "I don't want Comfort to be sick, and she sha'n't be if I can help it; but I've got a duty to her that's beyond looking out for her health. She's got a lesson to learn that's more important than any she's got in school, and I'm afraid she won't learn it at all unless she learns it by the hardest; and it won't do for me to help her."

"Well, I suppose you're right, Em'ly," said Grandmother Atkins; "but I declare I'm dreadfully sorry for the child."

"You ain't any sorrier than I am," said Comfort's mother. And she wiped her eyes now and then as she cleared away the breakfast dishes.

As for Comfort, she went on her way to school, looking as industriously and anxiously at the ground as if she were a little robin seeking for her daily food. Under the snowy blackberry-vines peered Comfort, under frozen twigs, and in the blue hollows of the snow, seeking, as it were, in the little secret places of nature for her own little secret of childish vanity and disobedience. It made no difference to her that it was not reasonable to look on that part of the road, since she could not have lost the ring there. She had a desperate hope, which was not affected by reason at all, and she determined to look everywhere.

It was very cold still, and when she came in sight of the school-house not a scholar was to be seen. Either they had not arrived, or were huddling over the red-hot stove inside.

Comfort trudged past the school-house and went down the road to the old Loomis place. She searched again every foot of the road, but there was no gleam of gold in its white, frozen surface. There was the cold sparkle of the frost-crystals, and that was all.

Comfort went back. At the turn of that road she saw Matilda Stebbins coming down the other. The pink tip of Matilda's nose, and her winking black eyes, just appeared above her red tippet.

"Hullo!" she sung out, in a muffled voice.

"Hullo!" responded Comfort, faintly.

Matilda looked at her curiously when she came up.

"What's the matter?" said she.

"Nothing," replied Comfort.

"I thought you acted funny. What have you been up that road for?"

Comfort walked along beside Matilda in silence.

"What have you been up that road for?" repeated Matilda.

"Won't you ever tell?" said Comfort.

"No, I won't:

    "Honest and true,
Black and blue,
Lay me down and cut me in two."

"Well, I've lost it."

Matilda knew at once what Comfort meant. "You ain't!" she cried, stopping short and opening wide eyes of dismay at Comfort over the red tippet.

"Yes, I have."

"Where'd you lose it?"

"I felt of my pocket after I got back to school yesterday, after we'd been up to the old Loomis house, and I couldn't find the ring."

"My!" said Matilda.

Comfort gave a stifled sob.

Matilda turned short around with a jerk. "Le'ss go up that road and hunt again," said she; "there's plenty of time before the bell rings. Come along, Comfort Pease."

So the two little girls went up the road and hunted, but they did not find the ring. "Nobody would have picked it up and kept it; everybody around here is honest," said Matilda. "It's dreadfully funny."

Comfort wept painfully under the folds of her mother's green shawl as they went back.

"Did your mother scold you?" asked Matilda. There was something very innocent and sympathizing and honest about Matilda's black eyes as she asked the question.

"No," faltered Comfort. She did not dare tell Matilda that her mother knew nothing at all about it.

Matilda, as they went along, put an arm around Comfort under her shawl. "Don't cry; it's too bad," said she. But Comfort wept harder.

"Look here," said Matilda. "Comfort, your mother wouldn't let you buy another ring with that gold dollar, would she?"

"That gold dollar's to keep," sobbed Comfort; "it ain't to spend." And, indeed, she felt as if spending that gold dollar would be almost as bad as losing the ring; the bare idea of it horrified her.

"Well, I didn't s'pose it was," said Matilda, abashedly. "I just happened to think of it." Suddenly she gave Comfort a little poke with her red-mittened hand. "Don't you cry another minute, Comfort Pease," she cried. "I'll tell you what I'll do. I'll ask my Uncle Jared to give me a gold dollar, and then I'll give it to you to buy a gold ring."

"I don't believe he will," sobbed Comfort.

"Yes, he will. He always gives me everything I ask him for. He thinks more of me than he does of Rosy and Imogen, you know, 'cause he was going to get married once, when he was young, and she died, and I look like her."

"Were you named after her?" inquired Comfort.

"No; her name was Ann Maria; but I look like her. Uncle Jared will give me a gold dollar, and I'll ask him to take us to Bolton in his sleigh Saturday afternoon, and then you can buy another ring. Don't you cry another mite, Comfort Pease."

And poor Comfort tried to keep the tears back as the bell began to ring, and she and Matilda hastened to the school-house.

Matilda put up her hand and whispered to her in school-time. "You come over to my house Saturday afternoon, and I'll get Uncle Jared to take us," she whispered. And Comfort nodded soberly. Comfort tried to learn her arithmetic lesson, but she could not remember the seven multiplication table, and said in the class that five times seven were fifty-seven, and went to the foot. She cried at that, and felt a curious satisfaction in having something to cry for besides the loss of the ring.

Comfort did not look any more for the ring that day nor the next. The next day was Friday, and Matilda met her at school in the morning with an air of triumph. She plunged her hand deep in her pocket, and drew it out closed in a tight pink fist. "Guess what I've got in here, Comfort Pease," said she. She unclosed her fingers a little at a time, until a gold dollar was visible in the hollow of her palm. "There, what did I tell you" she said. "And he says he'll take us to Bolton if he don't have to go to Ware to see about buying a horse. You come over to-morrow, right after dinner."

The next morning after breakfast Comfort asked her mother if she might go over to Matilda's that afternoon.

"Do you feel fit to go?" her mother said, with a keen look at her. Comfort was pale and sober and did not have much appetite. It had struck her several times that her mother's and also her grandmother's manner toward her was a little odd, but she did not try to understand it.

"Yes, ma'am," said Comfort.

"What are you going to do over there?"

Comfort hesitated. A pink flush came on her face and neck. Her mother's eyes upon her were sharper than ever. "Matilda said maybe her Uncle Jared would take us a sleigh-ride to Bolton," she faltered.

"Well," said her mother, "if you're going a sleigh-ride you'd better take some yarn stockings to pull over your shoes, and wear my fur tippet. It's most too cold to go sleigh-riding, anyway."

Directly after dinner Comfort went over to Matilda Stebbins's, with her mother's stone-marten tippet around her neck and the blue yarn stockings to wear in the sleigh under her arm.

But when she got to the Stebbins's house, Matilda met her at the door with a crestfallen air. "Only think," said she; "ain't it too bad? Uncle Jared had to go to Ware to buy the horse, and we can't go to Bolton."

Comfort looked at her piteously.

"Guess I'd better go home," said she.

But Matilda was gazing at her doubtfully. "Look here," said she.

"What?" said Comfort.

"It ain't mor'n three miles to Bolton. Mother's walked there, and so has Imogen—"

"Do you s'pose—we could?"

"I don't b'lieve it would hurt us one mite. Say, I tell you what we can do: I'll take my sled, and I'll drag you a spell and then you can drag me, and that will be riding half the way for both of us, anyhow."

"So it will," said Comfort.

But Matilda looked doubtful again. "There's only one thing," she said. "Mother ain't at home—she and Rosy went over to grandma's to spend the day this morning—and I can't ask her. I don't see how I can go without asking her, exactly."

Comfort thought miserably, "What would Matilda Stebbins say if she knew I took that ring when my mother told me not to?"

"Well," said Matilda, brightening, "I don't know but it will do just as well if I ask Imogen. Mother told me once that if there was anything very important came up when she was away that I could ask Imogen."

Imogen was Matilda's eldest sister. She was almost eighteen, and she was going to a party that night, and was hurrying to finish a beautiful crimson tibet dress to wear.

"Now don't you talk to me and hinder me one moment. I've everything I can do to finish this dress to wear to the party," she said, when Matilda and Comfort went into the sitting-room.

"Can't I go to Bolton with Comfort Pease, Imogen?" asked Matilda.

"I thought you were going with Uncle Jared—didn't mother say you might? Now don't talk to me, Matilda."

"Uncle Jared's got to go to Ware to buy the horse, and he can't take us."

"Oh, I forgot. Well, how can you go, then? You and Comfort had better sit down and play checkers, and be contented."

"We could walk," ventured Matilda.

"Walk to Bolton? You couldn't."

"It's only three miles, and we'd drag each other on my sled."

Imogen frowned over a wrong pucker in the crimson tibet, and did not appreciate the absurdity of the last. "I do wish you wouldn't bother me, Matilda," said she. "If I don't get this dress done I can't go to the party to-night. I don't know what mother would say to your going to Bolton any such way."

"It wouldn't hurt us a mite. Do let us go, Imogen."

"Well, I'll tell you what you can do," said Imogen. "You can walk over there—I guess it won't hurt you to walk one way—and then you can ride home in the stage-coach; it comes over about half-past four. I'll give you some money."

"Oh, that's beautiful! Thank you, Imogen," cried Matilda, gratefully.

"Well, run along and don't say another word to me," said Imogen, scowling over the crimson tibet. "Wrap up warm."

When they started, Matilda insisted upon dragging Comfort first in the sled. "I'll drag you as far as Dr. Hutchins's," said she. "Then you get off and drag me as far as the meeting-house. I guess that's about even."

It was arduous, and it is probable that the little girls were much longer reaching Bolton than they would have been had they traveled on their two sets of feet all the way; but they persuaded themselves otherwise.

"We can't be—a mite—tired," panted Matilda, as she tugged Comfort over the last stretch, "for we each of us rode half the way, and a mile and a half ain't anything. You walk that every day to school and back."

"Yes, I do," assented Comfort. She could not believe that she was tired, either, although every muscle in her body ached.

Bolton was a large town, and the people from all the neighboring villages went there to do their trading and shopping. There was a wide main street, with stores on each side; and that day it was full of sleighs and pungs and wood-sleds, and there were so many people that Comfort felt frightened. She had never been to Bolton without her father or mother. "Just look at all the folks," said she. And she had an uncomfortable feeling that they all stared at her suspiciously, although she did not see how they could know about the ring. But Matilda was bolder. "It's such a pleasant day that they're all out trading," said she. "Guess it'll storm to-morrow. Now we want to go to Gerrish's. I went there once with mother and Imogen to buy a silver spoon for Cousin Hannah Green when she got married."

Comfort, trailing the sled behind her, started timidly after Matilda.

Gerrish's was a small store, but there was a large window full of watches and chains and clocks, and a man with spectacles sat behind it mending watches.

The two little girls went in and stood at the counter, and a thin man with gray whiskers, who was Mr. Gerrish himself, came forward to wait upon them. Matilda nudged Comfort.

"You ask him—it's your ring," she whispered.

But Comfort shook her head. She was almost ready to cry. "You'd ought to when I'm giving you the dollar," whispered Matilda, with another nudge. Mr. Gerrish stood waiting, and he frowned a little; he was a nervous man. "Ask him," whispered Matilda, fiercely.

Suddenly Comfort Pease turned herself about and ran out of Gerrish's, with a great wail of inarticulate words about not wanting any ring. The door banged violently after her. Matilda Stebbins looked after her in a bewildered way; then she looked up at Mr. Gerrish, who was frowning harder. "If you girls don't want anything, you'd better stay out of doors with your sled," said he. And Matilda trembled and gathered up the sled-rope, and the door banged after her. Then Mr. Gerrish said something to the man mending watches in the window, and went back to his desk in the rear of the store.

Matilda could just see Comfort running down the street toward home, and she ran after her. She could run faster than Comfort. As she got nearer she could see people turning and looking curiously after Comfort, and when she came up to her she saw she was crying. "Why, you great baby, Comfort Pease," said she, "going along the road crying!"

Comfort sobbed harder, and people stared more and more curiously. Finally one stout woman in a black velvet bonnet stopped. "I hope you haven't done anything to hurt this other little girl?" she said, suspiciously, to Matilda.

"No, ma'am, I ain't," replied Matilda.

"What's the matter, child?" said the woman in the black velvet bonnet to Comfort. And Comfort choked out something about losing her ring.

"Where did you lose it?" asked the woman.

"I don't k—n—o—w," sobbed Comfort.

"Well, you'd better go right home and tell your mother about it," said the stout woman, and went her way with many backward glances.

Matilda dragged her sled to Comfort's side and eyed her dubiously.

"Why didn't you get the ring when we were right there with the gold dollar?" she demanded. "What made you run out of Gerrish's that way?"

"I'm—go—ing—home," sobbed Comfort.

"Ain't you going to wait and ride in the stage coach?"

"I'm—going—right—home."

"Imogen said to go in the stage-coach. I don't know as mother'll like it if we walk. Why didn't you get the ring, Comfort Pease?"

"I don't want—any—ring. I'm going home—to—tell—my mother."

"Your mother would have been real pleased to have you get the ring," said Matilda, in an injured tone; for she fancied Comfort meant to complain of her to her mother.

Then Comfort turned on Matilda in an agony of confession. "My mother don't know anything about it," said she. "I took the ring unbeknownst to her when she said I couldn't, and then I lost it, and I was going to get the new ring to put in the box so she wouldn't ever know. I'm going right home and tell her."

Matilda looked at her. "Comfort Pease, didn't you ask your mother?" said she.

Comfort shook her head.

"Then," said Matilda, solemnly, "we'd better go home just as quick as we can. We won't wait for any stage-coach—I know my mother wouldn't want me to. S'pose your mother should die, or anything, before you have a chance to tell her, Comfort Pease! I read a story once about a little girl that told a lie, and her mother died, and she hadn't owned up. It was dreadful. Now you get right on the sled, and I'll drag you as far as the meeting-house, and then you can drag me as far as the saw-mill."

Comfort huddled herself up on the sled in a miserable little bunch, and Matilda dragged her. Her very back looked censorious to Comfort, but finally she turned around.

"The big girls were real mean, so there; and they pestered you dreadfully," said she. "Don't you cry any more, Comfort. Just you tell your mother all about it, and I don't believe she'll scold much. You can have this gold dollar to buy you another ring, anyway, if she'll let you."

The road home from Bolton seemed much longer than the road there had done, although the little girls hurried, and dragged each other with fierce jerks. "Now," said Matilda, when they reached her house at length, "I'll go home with you while you tell your mother, if you want me to, Comfort. My mother's got home—I can see her head in the window. I'll run and ask her."

"I'd just as lief go alone, I guess," replied Comfort, who was not crying any more, but was quite pale. "I'm real obliged to you, Matilda."

"Well, I'd just as lief go as not, if you wanted me to," said Matilda. "I hope your mother won't say much. Good-by, Comfort."

"Good-by," returned Comfort.

Then Matilda went into her house, and Comfort hurried home alone down the snowy road in the deepening dusk. She kept thinking of that dreadful story which Matilda had read. She was panting for breath. Anxiety and remorse and the journey to Bolton had almost exhausted poor little Comfort Pease. She hurried as fast as she could, but her feet felt like lead, and it seemed to her that she should never reach home. But when at last she came in sight of the lighted kitchen windows her heart gave a joyful leap, for she saw her mother's figure moving behind them, and knew that Matilda's story was not true in her case.

When she reached the door she leaned against it a minute. She was so out of breath, and her knees seemed failing under her. Then she opened the door and went in.

Her father and mother and grandmother were all in there, and they turned round and stared at her.

"Comfort Pease," cried her mother, "what is the matter?"

"You didn't fall down, or anythin', did you?" asked her grandmother.

Then Comfort burst out with a great sob of confession. "I—took—it," she gasped. "I took my gold ring that Aunt Comfort gave me for her name—and—I wore it to school, and Miss Tabitha pinned it in my pocket, and I lost it. And Matilda she gave me the gold dollar her Uncle Jared gave her to buy me another, and we walked a mile and a half apiece to Bolton, to buy it in Gerrish's, and I couldn't; and I was afraid something had happened to mother; and I'm sorry." Then Comfort sobbed until her very sobs seemed failing her.

Her father wiped his eyes. "Don't let that child cry that way, Em'ly," said he to Mrs. Pease. Then he turned to Comfort. "Don't you feel so bad, Comfort," he coaxed. "Father'll get you some peppermints when he goes down to the store to-night." Comfort's father gave her a hard pat on her head; then he went out of the room with something that sounded like an echo of Comfort's own sobs.

"Comfort," said Mrs. Pease, "look here, child. Stop crying, and listen to what I've got to say. I want you to come into the parlor with me a minute."

Comfort followed her mother weakly into the best parlor. There on the table stood the rosewood work-box, and her mother went straight across to it and opened it.

"Look here, Comfort," said she; and Comfort looked. There in its own little compartment lay the ring. "Miss Tabitha Hanks found it in the road, and she thought you had taken it unbeknownst to me, and so she brought it here," explained her mother. "I didn't let you know because I wanted to see if you would be a good girl enough to tell me of your own accord, and I'm glad you have, Comfort."

Then Comfort's mother carried her almost bodily back to the warm kitchen and sat her before the fire to toast her feet, while she made some cream-toast for her supper.

Her grandmother had a peppermint in her pocket, and she slid it into Comfort's hand. "Grandma knew she would tell, and she won't never do such a thing again, will she?" said she.

"No, ma'am," replied Comfort. And the peppermint in her mouth seemed to be the very flavor of peace and forgiveness.

After Comfort was in bed and asleep that night her elders talked the matter over. "I knew she would tell finally," said Mrs. Pease; "but it's been a hard lesson for her, poor child, and she's all worn out—that long tramp to Bolton, too"

"I 'most wish her Aunt Comfort hadn't been so dreadful careful about getting her a ring big enough," said Grandmother Atkins.

Mr. Pease looked at his wife and cleared his throat. "What do you think of my getting her a ring that would fit her finger, Em'ly?" he asked, timidly.

"Now, father, that's all a man knows!" cried Mrs. Pease. "If you went and bought that child a ring now it would look just as if you were paying her for not minding. You'd spoil all the lesson she's got, when she's worked so dreadful hard to learn it. You wait awhile."

"Well, I suppose you know best, Em'ly," said Mr. Pease; but he made a private resolution. And so it happened that three months later, when it was examination day at school, and Comfort had a new blue tibet dress to wear, and some new ribbon to tie her hair, that her mother handed her a little box just before she started.

"Here," said she. "Your father has been over to Gerrish's, and here's something he bought you. I hope you'll be careful and not lose it."

And Comfort opened the box, and there was a beautiful gold ring, which just fitted her third finger; and she wore it to school, and the girls all seemed to see it at once, and exclaimed, "Comfort Pease has got a new gold ring that fits her finger!"

And that was not all, for Matilda and Rosy Stebbins also wore gold rings. "Mother said I might as well spend Uncle Jared's dollar for it, 'cause your mother didn't want you to have it," said Matilda, holding her finger up; "and father bought one for Rosy, too."

Then the two little girls took their seats, and presently went forward to be examined in spelling before the committee-men, the doctor, the minister, and all the visiting friends.

And Comfort Pease, with all the spelling lessons of the term in her head, her gold ring on her finger, and peace in her heart, went to the head of the class, and Miss Tabitha Hanks presented her with a prize. It was a green silk pincushion with "Good Girl" worked on it in red silk, and she had it among her treasures long after her finger had grown large enough to wear her Aunt Comfort's ring.